PATCHES
FINDS A NEW HOME

PATCHES
FINDS A NEW HOME

by EDNA MILLER

Simon and Schuster Books for Young Readers
Published by Simon & Schuster Inc.
New York

To

MEHUSHKA,

JINGLES,

PATCHES,

PRISSY,

and

FLEA

SIMON AND SCHUSTER
BOOKS FOR YOUNG READERS
Simon & Schuster Building
Rockefeller Center
1230 Avenue of the Americas
New York, New York 10020

SIMON AND SCHUSTER BOOKS FOR YOUNG READERS
is a trademark of Simon & Schuster Inc.
Manufactured in the U.S.A.

10 9 8 7 6 5 4 3 2 1

Library of Congress Cataloging-in-Publication Data
Miller, Edna, 1920–
Patches finds a new home.
SUMMARY: Patches, a tame tabby cat, raises her
kittens in the forest, until the approach of a
hurricane forces her to seek shelter at a roadside house.
[1. Cats—Fiction] I. Title.
PZ7.M6128Pat   1989   [E]   87-32355
ISBN 0-671-66266-X

WHEN Patches, a tame tabby–patch cat,
went hunting for food in the forest,
she made certain her two small kittens
were safely hid and fast asleep
inside a hollow log.

8662-CR

That day she hadn't gone far
from the hiding place
when she heard a kitten mee–ew.
Leaping back through briar and bush,
she saw what she feared most:
one kitten had wandered outside to play.
The other cried out loudly.

A hungry fox heard the kitten cry too.
He watched the other one play.

In an instant the tame tabby–patch
changed into a wild, fearful thing.
She gave a long, low growl.
Then hissing and spitting with rage,
teeth bared and fur raised on end,
she dashed at the startled intruder.
The fox wasn't that hungry,
and quietly slipped away.

The hollow log had been safe enough
for kittens newly born,
but now, with their bright eyes open wide,
they wanted to explore.
Foxes, weasels, hawks and owls
explore the forest too.

Patches knew the time had come
to bring her kittens home
to the house at the edge of the woods
she had left before they were born.
The big friendly dog and old tom cat
would no longer be a threat
to two small kittens with sharp teeth and claws,
able to scamper about.

When evening came and nothing stirred
but the sound of leaves in the wind,
Patches called her kittens
with soft trilling sounds.

Lifting one kitten in a gentle grip,
she followed a path she knew.
With low throaty calls and purring,
she coaxed the other to follow.

When the leafy mold of the forest floor
gave way to soft green grasses
and goldenrod and daisies grew in an open field,
Patches knew she was home.

But as she hurried through the open gate,
she sensed the house was empty.
Nothing stirred in the silence.
There was no one living there.
The dog was gone. The tom cat was gone,
and so was the saucer of milk.

Patches knew she must find a new home
before night fell.
There are foxes, weasels, hawks and owls
that hunt at the edge of the forest.
Carrying one kitten and then the other,
she followed a country road. At last,
when the katydids had begun their evening song,
she spied a lamp-lit window.

The little house sat near the edge of the road:
no fence or gate barred her way.
Near the house was a large stack of wood
—a hiding place for her kittens.

When morning came, her kittens fed,
Patches explored the porch.
There were pots of flowers,
and soft-cushioned chairs
like those she had known before.
Just as she settled into a chair
and began to clean her coat,
she heard a rap on the window
and someone inside shout, "Scat!"

Patches jumped from the cushioned chair
onto a wide porch railing.
As she continued to clean and preen,
she heard the cottage door open.
A hand reached out with a saucer of milk,
then quickly shut the door again.

Each morning the hand appeared at the door
and placed a saucer of milk outside.
Though it never reached out to stroke her fur,
Patches knew she was welcome.

While Patches went off hunting
moles and voles and rodents in the field,
her kittens played in the woodpile.
There were games of tag and hide–go–seek,
peek–a–boo and catch.

The kittens were too busy playing
to see the cottage curtains part,
or hear the laughter from inside.

With saucers of milk and food from the field
to feed her hungry kittens,
Patches had nothing to fear—
'til one bright and cloudless day
she sensed something more frightening
than any fox, weasel, hawk or owl—
she sensed a fearful storm. A hurricane.
Circling the house, she found an open window.
Patches knew she must bring her kittens inside.

Beneath the window a flight of stairs
led down to a small dark room.
There were shelves of jars and tins of things
for her kittens to explore.
When one of the jars crashed to the floor,
a voice cried out, "Who's there?"
Patches raced for the open window;
her kittens followed later.

Patches called to her kittens.
She hurried back to the open window
and dropped the two inside.
This time she found a room
at the top of the stairs,
and a safe, warm place to hide.

Cat and kittens were fast asleep
when the coverlet was snatched away.
"Out! Out!" Patches heard
as she raced for the open window.
Once again her kittens were shown the door!

The next morning there was no saucer of milk.
Patches comforted her kittens near the woodpile.
They too sensed the danger in the still autumn air
and cuddled close to their mother.

Near dusk Patches spied the door ajar.
In an instant cat and kittens raced
through the opening and scooted
beneath a large overstuffed chair.
The door slammed shut and the first
drops of rain splashed against
the windowpane.
Wind whistled through the leafy
branches outside.

Rain pelted down. A green lightning
lit the sky, making eerie shadows
dance upon the wall.
Above the wailing of the wind
Patches heard a voice near the woodpile call,
"Kitty! Here Kitty, Kitty!"

Shutters creaked on their hinges,
slamming open and shut in the gusting wind.
Above the raging storm,
Patches heard the voice far off
calling, "Kitty, Kitty, Kitty!"

. . . . and farther still, "Here Kitty."

Only the tick of the mantel clock
and the crackle of logs on the fire
answered the calls outside.
Patches knew she had found a new home.